ISAAC ASIMOV'S NEW LIBRARY OF THE UNIVERSE

FOLKLORE AND LEGENDS OF THE UNIVERSE

BY ISAAC ASIMOV

WITH REVISIONS AND UPDATING BY FRANCIS REDDY

Gareth Stevens Publishing
MILWAUKEE

For a free color catalog describing Gareth Stevens' list of high-quality books, call 1-800-542-2595 (USA) or 1-800-461-9120 (Canada). Gareth Stevens' Fax: (414) 225-0377.

Library of Congress Cataloging-in-Publication Data

Asimov, Isaac.
  Folklore and legends of the universe / by Isaac Asimov; with
revisions and updating by Francis Reddy.
      p. cm. — (Isaac Asimov's New library of the universe)
  Rev. ed. of: Mythology and the universe. 1990.
  Includes index.
  Summary: Presents beliefs of ancient peoples about the universe.
  ISBN 0-8368-1234-4
  1. Astronomy—Folklore—Juvenile literature. [1. Astronomy—
Folklore.] I. Reddy, Francis, 1959-. II. Asimov, Isaac. Mythology
and the universe. III. Title. IV. Series: Asimov, Isaac. New library
of the universe.
QB46.A783 1996
523.1—dc20   95-40363

This edition first published in 1996 by
Gareth Stevens Publishing
1555 North RiverCenter Drive, Suite 201
Milwaukee, Wisconsin 53212, USA

Project editor: Barbara J. Behm
Design adaptation: Helene Feider
Editorial assistant: Diane Laska
Production director: Teresa Mahsem
Picture research: Matthew Groshek and Diane Laska

Printed in the United States of America

1 2 3 4 5 6 7 8 9 99 98 97 96

To bring this classic of young people's information up to date, the editors at Gareth Stevens Publishing have selected two noted science authors, Greg Walz-Chojnacki and Francis Reddy. Walz-Chojnacki and Reddy coauthored the recent book *Celestial Delights: The Best Astronomical Events Through 2001.*

Walz-Chojnacki is also the author of the book *Comet: The Story Behind Halley's Comet* and various articles about the space program. He was an editor of *Odyssey,* an astronomy and space technology magazine for young people, for eleven years.

Reddy is the author of nine books, including *Halley's Comet, Children's Atlas of the Universe, Children's Atlas of Earth Through Time,* and *Children's Atlas of Native Americans,* plus numerous articles. He was an editor of *Astronomy* magazine for several years.

CONTENTS

We live in an enormously large place – the Universe. It's just in the last fifty-five years or so that we've found out how large it probably is. It's only natural that we would want to understand the place in which we live, so scientists have developed instruments – such as radio telescopes, satellites, probes, and many more – that have told us far more about the Universe than could possibly be imagined.

We have seen planets up close. We have learned about quasars and pulsars, black holes, and supernovas. We have gathered amazing data about how the Universe may have come into being and how it may end. Nothing could be more astonishing.

But in ancient times, people looked at the sky with only their eyes – and were in complete awe over what they saw. They created stories about their observations of the sky that helped them make sense of it all. Many of these stories, now folklore and legends, influence our view of the Universe to this very day.

Isaac Asimov

Sun Worship

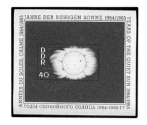

The Sun gives us light and warmth. Near Earth's Equator, the Sun remains high in the sky. But farther north or south, the Sun is sometimes low in the sky. When this happens, the days become shorter and cooler, and winter comes. Winter is a reminder that, without the Sun, there would be only darkness and freezing cold. The ancients pictured the Sun as a glorious and good god.

Ancient Greeks imagined the Sun god, Helios, driving a flaming chariot across the sky. The Babylonians said the Sun god, Shamash, provided laws for people to follow. The Egyptian Sun god, Ra, was considered the nation's protector. One king of Egypt, Akhenaton, thought the Sun god was the only god.

Ancient peoples had various images of the Sun: from Europe in the Middle Ages *(above)*; a dragon below the fiery Sun from eighteenth-century China *(below)*; and the great eye of Ra, Sun god of the ancient Egyptians *(opposite, top)*.

Opposite, bottom: A time-lapse photo of the Sun in the Arctic.

? Does Sirius cause the "dog days" of summer?

The sky's brightest star, Sirius, is in the constellation of Canis Major (Great Dog). Canis Major is near the constellation of Orion (the Hunter), so it is said to be the Hunter's dog. Ancient Greeks thought Sirius was so bright that it must deliver heat to Earth like a smaller Sun. And when Sirius and our Sun were in the sky together, they both supposedly gave the Northern Hemisphere its intense midsummer heat. This is not true, but we do call this hot period of summer the "dog days."

Moon Cycles

The Moon appears much dimmer than the Sun. In myths, it is usually pictured as a gentle female. To the ancient Greeks, she was Selene. To the Egyptians, she was Isis.

The Moon changes its appearance, going through a cycle each month from a thin crescent to a full moon and back to a thin crescent. Ancient calendars were based on this monthly cycle, and twelve of the cycles made up a year.

As a matter of fact, both the word *month* and the word *Monday* come from the word *moon*.

Opposite, top: This red moon "monster" was drawn on the shield of a Crow Indian.

Top: The ancient Greeks pictured the Moon as a beautiful maiden, Selene.

Right: This special watch shows the phases of the Moon

Opposite, bottom: For as long as people have gazed at the Moon, they have imagined pictures on its face. Look for the "maiden" *(right)*, the "rabbit" *(center)*, and the "man in the moon" *(left)*.

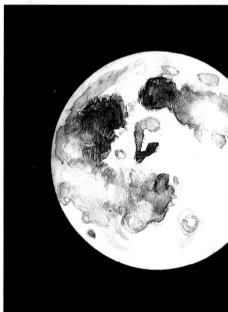

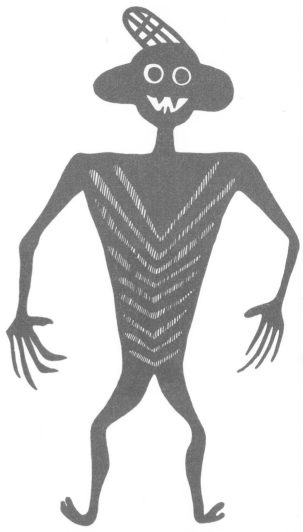

Wanderers of the Sky

From day to day and night to night, the Sun and Moon change their positions against the stars. In addition, the ancients spotted five bright starlike objects, called planets, that also moved across the sky. The word *planet* comes from the Greek word for "wanderer." The ancient Babylonians observed the night sky and watched the planets travel across the sky. They named the planets after gods.

The brightest planet in the sky is Venus, named for the goddess of beauty. A red planet the color of blood is Mars, named after the god of war. The fastest-moving planet is Mercury, named after the messenger of the gods. The slowest planet known in ancient times was Saturn, named for the god of agriculture. The second brightest planet in the sky, Jupiter, was named for the chief god. Jupiter is not as bright as Venus, but it shines all night; Venus appears only in the evening or at dawn.

Opposite, top: This ancient Babylonian view of the Universe shows a disk of land with water all around. Babylonia is shown at the center of the disk.

Opposite, bottom: Could this have been an ancient observatory? A story in the Bible tells how the people of a Babylonian city tried to build a stairway to the stars – the Tower of Babel.

Right: Ancient Chinese names for the four brightest planets *(top to bottom)*: Water Star – Mercury, Gold Star – Venus, Fire Star – Mars, and Wood Star – Jupiter.

The "New" Planets

In modern times, scientists have discovered three additional planets that are too far away from Earth for the ancients to have seen without special instruments. These planets have been named after gods, too.

Beyond Saturn is Uranus, named for the god of the sky, who was Saturn's father. Then there is Neptune, a sea-green planet named for the god of the sea. Beyond Neptune is Pluto, named for the god of the underworld because it is so far from the light of the Sun.

Satellites and asteroids are also named for figures from mythology, or the traditional stories about the gods. For example, Neptune's satellite is named for the god's son, Triton. In 1801, the first asteroid in the asteroid belt between Mars and Jupiter was discovered. It was named Ceres, after the goddess of agriculture. Other celestial bodies, such as Charon (Pluto's tiny moon); Leda and Io (both moons of Jupiter); Atlas, Prometheus, and Phoebe (moons of Saturn); and Juno, Eros, and Pallas (asteroids), are also named after mythological figures.

! Name that planet!

In 1930, a new observatory finally enabled astronomers to find Pluto. They realized that Pluto is so far from the Sun that it receives only dim light. For this reason, an eleven-year-old English girl suggested this planet be named after Pluto, god of the dark underworld. Also, "PL," the first letters of Pluto, are the initials of Percival Lowell, the man who built the observatory from where Pluto was first seen.

Left: In Greek mythology, Charon ferried the souls of the dead across the Styx River and into the underworld of Pluto. In 1978, when a moon was discovered orbiting the planet Pluto, the name *Charon* fit the new world perfectly.

Below, left: Pluto, god of the underworld, in the kingdom of death.

Below, right: Percival Lowell, the astronomer who began the search for a planet beyond Neptune.

Creatures Hiding the Light

Every so often, something unusual happens in the sky – the Sun or Moon is eclipsed, or blocked from view. The Sun is eclipsed when the Moon moves in front of it and hides its light. The Moon is eclipsed when it moves into Earth's shadow.

Ancient peoples didn't know the scientific reasons for these occurrences, so they invented reasons of their own. Some thought the Sun and Moon were chased by wolves, dragons, or other creatures that caught up with them now and then and started to swallow them. People would shout and bang drums to scare the creatures away and bring back the Sun and Moon.

Of course, the Sun and Moon have always come back from their eclipses. And they continue to do so, even though, according to Norse myths, a giant wolf will finally swallow them.

! *Meteorites – a big hit!*

Every once in a while, a "shooting star" can be seen in the sky. Some people think shooting stars fall, but they are actually meteoroids that streak through Earth's atmosphere and become what are known as meteors. In some cases, they even strike Earth and are called meteorites. Ancient peoples thought meteorites were holy objects. The Black Stone in the Kaaba, which Muslims consider holy, is probably a meteorite. But scientists are not allowed to study it, so nobody really knows for certain.

Opposite, left: According to Norse myths, at the end of the world, a giant wolf will swallow the Sun and Moon.

Opposite, top: During a lunar eclipse, the Moon's bright face turns a dusky red as it slips into Earth's shadow.

Opposite, bottom: In one Hindu story, the dragon Rahu causes an eclipse whenever he catches the Sun or Moon.

The Impending Doom of Comets

Comets are hazy objects with long tails. With a little imagination, they might look like a person's head with long, streaming hair. In fact, the word *comet* comes from the Greek word for "hair." At times, comets look like swords, so ancient peoples had reason to think of them as unpleasant omens. Most ancients thought comets were messages sent by the gods, warning of war, plague, and destruction. People would pray or ring church bells in order to try to ward off the evil.

But evil always came when there were comets in the sky. Of course, evil always came when comets were *not* in the sky, too – but people somehow didn't notice that!

! *More bark than bite!*

Comet tails contain poison gases, but the tails are so thin that the poison in them can't hurt anyone. In 1910, Earth was about to pass through the tail of Halley's Comet. Astronomers assured people there was no danger, but many people panicked anyway, thinking they would be poisoned and die. Some scoundrels sold phony pills that they said would prevent comet poisoning. Of course, that danger did not exist in the first place.

Above: This drawing of the "Great War Comet" from 1861 bears a resemblance to Jefferson Davis, president of the Confederate States of America.

Opposite: Comet West blazed through the winter skies in 1976. *Inset:* In earlier times, comets were often pictured as swordlike omens of war or disaster.

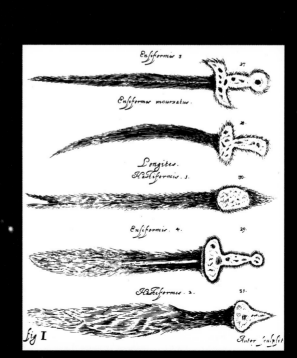

Constellations – Stars Together

When you look at the stars for a while, you'll find some that together form patterns. For instance, one group of stars in the northern sky can look like a *3*, an *E*, an *M*, or a *W*, depending on when you observe these stars. Ancient peoples associated star patterns with objects familiar to them, such as tools, animals, gods, and their heroes.

Some of these patterns, mainly those developed by the Greeks and Romans, were recognized by astronomers as a handy way of dividing the sky into eighty-eight different areas. These areas are called *constellations* – a word that means "stars together."

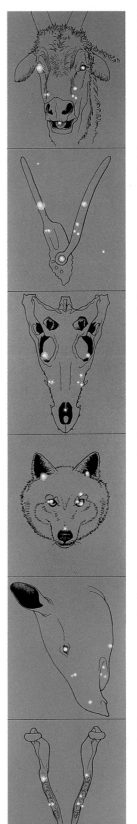

Bull
(Greek and Roman)

Nutcracker
(Indonesia)

Crocodile skull
(New Guinea)

Wolf
(Germany)

Tapir
(South America)

Bull's jaw
(Babylonia)

Opposite: The constellation Orion can be seen from the Northern Hemisphere. The traditional view of Orion is based on a Greek myth about a great hunter *(top, left)*. Orion has come to have different forms in various cultures. To the ancient Egyptians, Orion was Osiris, the God of Light, sailing down the Nile River *(top, right)*. To the ancient Japanese, the two brightest stars of Orion represented two samurai warriors. Separated by the constellation's central three stars, the warriors are about to engage in combat *(bottom, left)*. To the Borono Indians of Brazil, Orion is Jabuti, the Turtle *(bottom, right)*.

Right: The constellation Taurus can be seen northwest of Orion, high above the southern horizon. It is one of the oldest constellations mentioned in ancient historical accounts. It was seen as various animals and objects by different cultures.

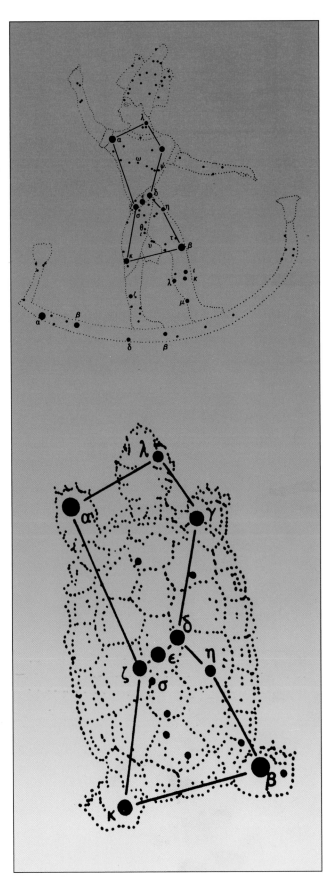

The Zodiac

It didn't take long for ancient peoples to realize that the Sun, Moon, and planets never strayed from a single belt wrapped all the way around the sky. The ancients divided this belt into twelve constellations, which then became the twelve months of the lunar calendar. The Sun took one month to pass through each constellation. When the Sun had moved through all twelve constellations, a year had passed.

Most of these constellations were pictured as animals. So the band in which the Sun, Moon, and the planets (except Pluto) move is known as the "circle of animals" – or zodiac.

Astronomers believe the zodiac was invented by the Babylonians of the Middle East nearly four thousand years ago. From there, it made its way to Egypt, Greece, China, and eventually to other countries and cultures.

Top to bottom: The rat, monkey, and rooster – three animals from the Japanese zodiac.

Opposite: A thirteenth-century artist pictures the month of May. The Sun moves on a wagon driven by winged horses from the constellation Taurus (the Bull) into Gemini (the Twins).

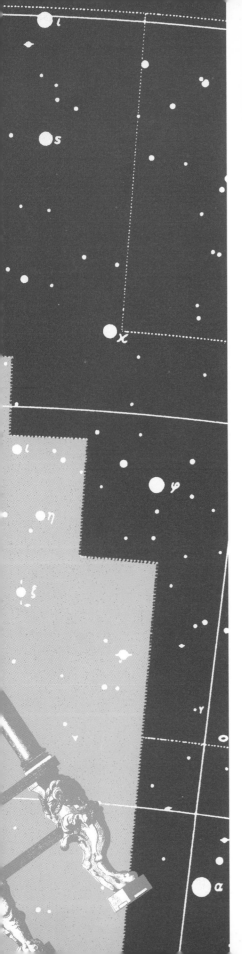

The Southern Sky

Some constellations can be seen only from the Southern Hemisphere. As seafaring explorers from Europe sailed farther from their homelands, they found themselves looking at new and unfamiliar stars. Astronomers charted these new stars in detail from observatories in South Africa in the seventeenth and eighteenth centuries. They recognized new constellations by "connecting the dots" – just as people had done for thousands of years. But the images used for these modern star patterns often seemed more technological than mythological. That's why the Southern Hemisphere has constellations such as Antlia (Air Pump), Pyxis (the Compass), and Horologium (the Clock).

Left: As Western sailors viewed the skies of the Southern Hemisphere, they recognized new constellations, such as Horologium, the Clock.

Below: With the help of a device called a sextant and mathematical calculations, sailors can find their location on Earth by observing the positions of the Sun and stars.

The Milky Way

Another part of the starry sky is the glow of our Galaxy, the Milky Way. The Milky Way is an irregular band of thick and distant stars. From Earth, it looks like a glowing mist.

In ancient times, the Milky Way was often seen as a road, river, or bridge along which spirits of the dead left the land of the living. For some American Indians, the stars in the Milky Way were campfires where souls could rest on their long journey. The Babylonians and ancient Mongols viewed the Milky Way as a seam joining the two halves of heaven. They thought light from the palaces of the gods could be seen through tiny holes in the stitching.

The Inca Indians of Peru imagined constellations within the band of the Milky Way. The dark clouds of dust that, in places, obscure the Milky Way's light became "dark constellations," such as the Fox, Llama, and Snake.

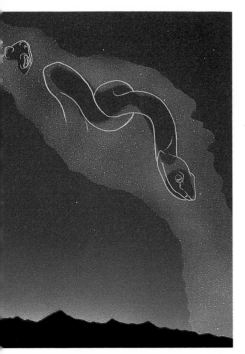

Opposite: The summer Milky Way from the constellations Cygnus to Sagittarius. Dark clouds of dust obscure some of the Milky Way's light.

Inset: The Incas recognized various constellations in the Milky Way's dark stretches of dust.

23

Polaris – the North Star

In the Northern Hemisphere, travelers have been guided for thousands of years by Polaris, the North Star.

From Europe, North America, and northern Asia, the constellations closest to Polaris never set. The Big Dipper, for example, just seems to spin around the sky. It changes positions throughout the night and over the year, but it's always above the horizon. For this reason, the Norse and the Mongols imagined Polaris as a spike that the heavens whirled around. The Chinese thought of it as an emperor, a chief star that ruled the others.

Polaris won't always be the North Star, nor has it always been. Over the coming centuries, Earth's axis will gradually point to different parts of the sky because the axis slowly wobbles.

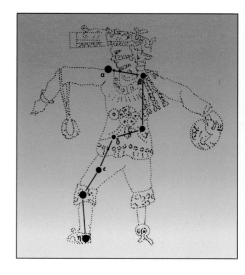

Above: The Big Dipper is one of the best-known star patterns. The Aztecs of Mexico saw their troublesome god Tezcatlipoca in the stars of the Big Dipper. Legend has it that another god was fed up with the problems Tezcatlipoca caused. This god turned Tezcatlipoca into a puppet and placed him in the sky, where he was forced to dance endlessly around Polaris.

Opposite, top: Ancient Romans saw the Big Dipper as the Seven Ploughing Oxen. The two stars at the front of the Dipper's bowl point toward Polaris.

Opposite, center: The Big Dipper is a part of the constellation Ursa Major (the Great Bear).

Opposite, bottom: The Wagon, a Babylonian version of the Big Dipper.

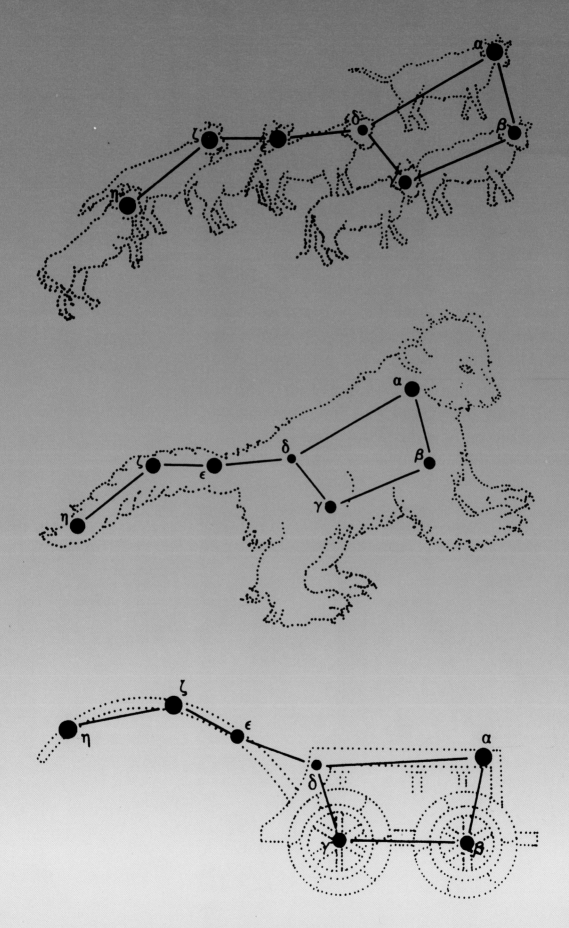

Endless Exploration

As you can see, people tell stories about the objects in the sky in different ways. Astronomers talk about the skies in scientific ways. Astrologers have developed methods for predicting the future by using the positions of the planets in the zodiac. This practice is called astrology.

Most scientists are skeptical about astrology, but many people believe it to be a true science, just as ancient peoples found their stories of the skies to be true.

History shows that while secrets of the Universe are still being uncovered, one thing remains certain – our endless desire to explore and make sense of the skies above us.

! The demon star – look only if you dare!

Perseus, a hero in Greek mythology, killed Medusa, an evil being with snakes in her hair. Legend has it that people turned to stone just looking at her. The constellation Perseus appears to hold the head of Medusa. One bright star stands out in her "head." It brightens and dims. The ancients called it the Demon Star. The Arabs named it Algol (the Ghoul), which is its name today.

Left: Astrologers have claimed throughout time that stars and planets influence our moods and fortunes. Even today, every major newspaper carries a horoscope *(opposite)* for those who seek advice from the stars.

Horoscope

Find your birthdate, and get some advice from the stars!

≈ Aquarius

Birthdate: January 20 - February 19
Look for and talk with those who share your interests. Some great insights will be revealed to you.

⯑ Pisces

Birthdate: February 20 - March 20
Be suspicious of people who appear to share your interests. They may be trying to take advantage of you.

♈ Aries

Birthdate: March 21 - April 19
Don't be discouraged by mistakes you make today. With a little patience, everything will work out fine.

♉ Taurus

Birthdate: April 20 - May 20
Listen to people carefully today. Their advice could be quite valuable.

♊ Gemini

Birthdate: May 21 - June 20
People may say nice things about you today. They may want something from you.

♋ Cancer

Birthdate: June 21 - July 22
Make plans for a long automobile trip.

♌ Leo

Birthdate: July 23 - August 22
Money could be available for you to start your own business.

♍ Virgo

Birthdate: August 23 - September 22
Someone may give you a chance to spend a sizable sum of money today. Be cautious and think it over before taking the plunge.

♎ Libra

Birthdate: September 23 - October 23
There are people less fortunate than you. Today, you will know where to find them. Do what you can for them.

♏ Scorpio

Birthdate: October 24 - November 22
A good day to be with friends. Find as many as you can with birthdays close to yours and celebrate together.

♐ Sagittarius

Birthdate: November 23 - December 21
Don't confuse people by rushing around. It is a good stay-at-home day. Bake something sweet.

♑ Capricorn

Birthdate: December 22 - January 19
Be on the move today. Don't stay in one place for long. Keep people guessing.

27

Fact File: The Changing Sky

Sometimes it is hard to imagine what ancient stargazers had in mind when they named the star patterns visible from Earth. For example, did the Greeks really see the figure of the mythological hunter Orion in a constellation that can look more like the figure of an hourglass? The fact is that people name things for many reasons. If a group of stars looks like a telescope, it might be named after a telescope. But sometimes it might be named to honor folklore and legends or to honor certain events or people, both real and mythological. After all, areas of land on Earth are named for similar reasons. It would be unusual if a city or state named *Washington* actually looked like a profile of George Washington.

There are also many reasons why the names, shapes, and legends of certain constellations have disappeared. Sometimes, over the course of centuries, the stars shift enough to move out of old patterns and into new ones. Sometimes a rich and thriving culture is conquered or disappears. Perhaps later generations simply choose to ignore a name that seems too sentimental. Or maybe a constellation does not disappear but is merely renamed, like *Andromeda*.

None of the constellation names in these illustrations or the chart is used any longer to describe our ever-changing sky.

Above and opposite:
Three constellations that have vanished: Bufo (the Toad), Aranca (the Spider), and the Archangel Gabriel.

Constellations of the Past

NAME	COMMENTS
Tiamat	Named by the Babylonians to represent the Great Mother who was murdered by her grandson for plotting to overthrow the gods. Like many constellations, Tiamat was "borrowed" from the Babylonians by the ancient Greeks. Today, it is known as Andromeda. Andromeda's story is about her rescue from a monster named Cetus (another constellation) by the Greek hero Perseus (also one of the constellations).
Mons Maenalus	Named in 1679 for the mountain home of the Greek god Pan.
Bufo (the Toad)	Named in 1768 by John Hill, an eccentric English physician. It is composed of a noticeable cluster of stars near the constellations Scorpio and Libra.
Limax (the Slug)	Also named in 1768 by John Hill. The constellation represents a snail without its shell. Most of the stars in this extinct constellation are toward the head and lower parts of the body, with few in the middle.
Felis (the Cat)	Named in 1799 by J. J. L. de Lalande, a person who loved cats. The name has not been used since the nineteenth century.
Officina Typographica (the Printing Office)	Named in 1799 to honor the invention of the printing press (Southern Hemisphere).
Telescopium Herschel II	Named in 1781 to honor the German-born English astronomer who discovered Uranus.
Circle of Chiefs	Named by the Skidi Pawnee Indians, who once arranged their villages in patterns that duplicated the positions of their most important star gods in the sky. Represents Tirawahat, the central force of the Universe.
Seven Boys Transformed into Geese	Named by the Chumash Indians of California. This constellation is now known in North America as the Big Dipper.

More Books about Folklore and Legends of the Universe

Astro-Dome Book: 3-D Map of the Night Sky. Hunig (Constellation)
Astronomy in Ancient Times. Asimov (Gareth Stevens)
Find the Constellations. Rey (Houghton Mifflin)
Night Sky. Barrett (Franklin Watts)
Outer Space. Jobes (Scarecrow)
A Stargazer's Guide. Asimov (Gareth Stevens)
Words from the Myths. Asimov (New American Library)

Videos

Ancient Astronomy. (Gareth Stevens)
Mythology and the Universe. (Gareth Stevens)

Places to Visit

You can explore the Universe without leaving Earth. Here are some museums and centers where you can find a variety of space exhibits.

National Air and Space Museum
Smithsonian Institution
Seventh and Independence Avenue SW
Washington, D.C. 20560

The Space and Rocket Center
    and Space Camp
One Tranquility Base
Huntsville, AL 35807

Australian Museum
6-8 College Street
Sydney, NSW 2000 Australia

Edmonton Space and Science Centre
11211 - 142nd Street
Edmonton, Alberta T5M 4A1

International Women's Air and Space Museum
One Chamber Plaza
Dayton, OH 45402

San Diego Aero-Space Museum
2001 Pan American Plaza-Balboa Park
San Diego, CA 92101

Places to Write

Here are some places you can write for more information about the Universe. Be sure to state what kind of information you would like. Include your full name and address for a reply.

National Space Society
922 Pennsylvania Avenue SE
Washington, D.C. 20003

Sydney Observatory
P. O. Box K346
Haymarket 2000 Australia

Jet Propulsion Laboratory
Teacher Resource Center
4800 Oak Grove Drive
Pasadena, CA 91109

Canadian Space Agency
Communications Department
6767 Route de L'Aeroport
Saint Hubert, Quebec J3Y 8Y9

Glossary

asteroid: very small planets made of rock or metal. Thousands of asteroids exist in our Solar System, and they mainly orbit the Sun in large numbers between Mars and Jupiter. Some appear elsewhere in our Solar System – as meteoroids or possibly as "captured" moons of planets, such as Mars.

astrology: the study of the positions of the stars and planets and their supposed influence upon humans and events on Earth.

astronomer: a person involved in the scientific study of the Universe and its various bodies.

calendar: a system for dividing time, most commonly into days, weeks, and months. Every calendar has a starting day and ending day for the year.

Ceres: the Roman goddess of agriculture; the first asteroid to be discovered (1801).

comet: an object made of ice, rock, and gas. It has a vapor tail that may be seen when the comet's orbit brings it close to the Sun.

constellation: a grouping of stars in the sky that seems to trace a familiar figure or symbol. Constellations are named after something they appear to resemble.

"dog days": the period between early July and early September when the hot weather of summer usually occurs in the Northern Hemisphere.

eclipse: the partial or complete blocking of light from one astronomical body by another.

Halley's Comet: a comet that passes by Earth every 75-76 years. Named for English astronomer Edmund Halley, it is notable in that every pass by this comet has been documented since its first recorded sighting by the Chinese in 240 B.C. Its last pass occurred in 1986.

meteor: a meteoroid that has entered Earth's atmosphere. Also, the bright streak of light made as the meteoroid enters or moves through the atmosphere.

meteorite: a meteoroid that strikes Earth.

meteoroid: a lump of rock or metal drifting through space. Meteoroids can be as big as asteroids or as small as specks of dust.

Milky Way: the glowing mist of stars that is our Galaxy.

mythology: the traditional stories about the gods and legendary heroes of a group of people.

shooting star: a meteor that appears as a temporary streak of light in the night sky.

underworld: in Greek mythology, the place where it was believed people went when they died.

Ursa Major: "Great Bear"; a constellation near the North Star containing the stars that form the Big Dipper.

zodiac: the band of constellations across the sky that represents the paths of the Sun, the Moon, and the planets (except Pluto).

Index

Born in 1920, Isaac Asimov came to the United States as a young boy from his native Russia. As a young man, he was a student of biochemistry. In time, he became one of the most productive writers the world has ever known. His books cover a spectrum of topics, including science, history, language theory, fantasy, and science fiction. His brilliant imagination gained him the respect and admiration of adults and children alike. Sadly, Isaac Asimov died shortly after the publication of the first edition of *Isaac Asimov's Library of the Universe*.

The publishers wish to thank the following for permission to reproduce copyright and other material: front cover, Matthew Groshek and Kate Kriege/© Gareth Stevens, Inc., 1989; 4 (upper right), copyright-free reproduction from Ridley's *A Short Treatise of Magnetic Bodies and Motions*; 4-5, 5 (upper), Michael Holford; 5 (lower), © Forrest Baldwin; 6 (lower), Matthew Groshek/© Gareth Stevens, Inc., 1989; 6-7 (upper), Michael Holford; 6-7 (lower), Rick Karpinski/DeWalt and Associates 1989; 7 (upper), copyright-free reproduction of a Crow Indian shield, *circa* 1804; 7 (lower, both), Rick Karpinski/DeWalt and Associates 1989; 9 (upper), Mary Evans Picture Library; 9 (lower), Kunsthistorisches Museum; 11 (upper), Mary Evans Picture Library; 11 (lower left), © Keith Ward 1989; 11 (lower right), Lowell Observatory; 12 (left), Rick Karpinski/DeWalt and Associates 1989; 12 (upper), © Matthew Groshek 1986; 12 (lower), Rick Karpinski/DeWalt and Associates 1989; 14 (right), Historical Pictures Service, Chicago; 15 (large), © John Laborde 1976; 15 (inset), Adler Planetarium, Chicago; 16 (right, all), © Sally Bensusen 1989; 17 (upper and lower right), Julius D. W. Staal, 1988. *The New Patterns in the Sky: Myths and Legends of the Stars*. The McDonald & Woodward Publishing Company, Blacksburg, Virginia; 17 (lower left), Rick Karpinski/DeWalt and Associates 1989; 18 (right, all), © Matthew Powell 1989; 19, Giraudon/Art Resource, New York; 20-21, © Gareth Stevens, Inc., 1989; 21 (lower), Mary Evans Picture Library; 22, © Fred Espenak; 22-23, © Sally Bensusen; 24 (right), 25 (all), Julius D. W. Staal, 1988. *The New Patterns in the Sky: Myths and Legends of the Stars*. The McDonald & Woodward Publishing Company, Blacksburg, Virginia; 26 (lower), Matthew Groshek/© Gareth Stevens, Inc., 1989; 27, Ann Ronan Picture Library; 28-29 (all), Adler Planetarium, Chicago; 4 (upper left), 6 (upper), 8 (upper), 10, 13 (both), 14 (left), 16 (left), 18 (left), 21 (upper), 23, 24 (left), 26 (upper), 28 (postage stamps), from the collection of George G. Young, Astronomy Study Unit of the American Topical Association.